Henry Holt and Company, *Publishers since 1866*
Henry Holt® is a registered trademark of Macmillan Publishing Group, LLC
175 Fifth Avenue, New York, NY 10010 · mackids.com

Library of Congress Cataloging-in-Publication Data is available.
ISBN 978-1-62779-270-7

Our books may be purchased in bulk for promotional, educational, or
business use. Please contact your local bookseller or the Macmillan Corporate
and Premium Sales Department at (800) 221-7945 ext. 5442 or
by e-mail at MacmillanSpecialMarkets@macmillan.com.

First edition, 2018 / Designed by April Ward and Sophie Erb
The illustrations for this book were digitally painted and collaged in Adobe Photoshop.
Printed in China by Toppan Leefung Printing Ltd., Dongguan City, Guangdong Province
1 3 5 7 9 10 8 6 4 2

For Tony Webb,
builder extraordinaire

BUNNY BUILT

MICHAEL SLACK

Christy Ottaviano Books

Henry Holt and Company · New York

LaRue was the handiest bunny in Westmore Oaks.

He had everything an industrious bunny could ever need.

Everything, that is,
except carrots.

He checked all of his usual hiding spots.

He was completely out.

TOOT TOOT

So off he went to find some.

He stopped to ask Stella. "Do you have any carrots?"

"Afraid not. They were swept away when the wind blew down my house."

He stopped to ask Nevil. "Do you have any carrots?"
"Nope. They were in my boat but it sank."

He stopped to ask Ivy. "Do you have any carrots?"
"Sorry, LaRue. No carrots."
"What happened to your table?" Nevil asked Ivy.
"I gave it to Beaver. He needed wood to fix his dam.
But I found this beautiful rock to sit on."

"This is not a rock. It smells like carrots. Maybe it's a seed," LaRue said.
Everyone chuckled. Everyone had an idea.
"You can have it, LaRue," said Ivy.

LaRue's friends helped him load the orange ball into his dump truck.

When he got home, LaRue went straight to work.

He **dug**.

He **dumped**.

He **dozed**.

He **doused**.

He waited.

Then he brought in
the heavy equipment.

The crane creaked.

Pulleys pulled.

The ground shook and . . .

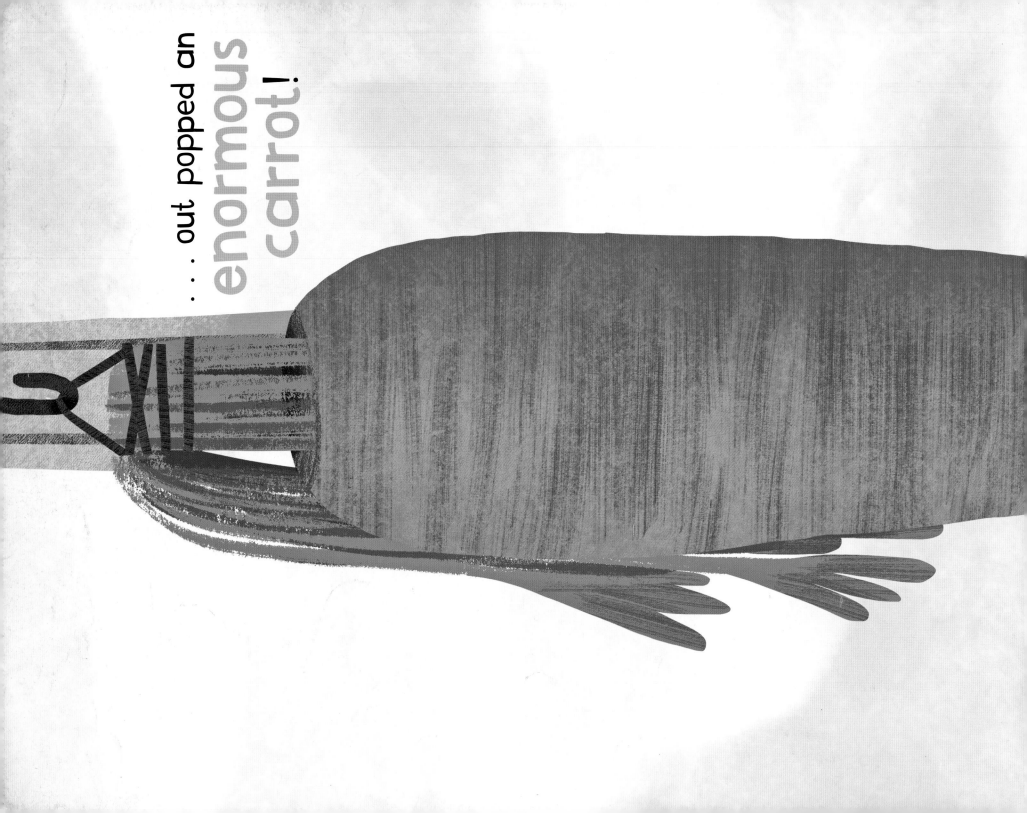

. . . out popped an **enormous carrot!**

"Whoa! What should I do with
all that carrot?" said LaRue.
Everyone had an idea.
But LaRue's idea was the best.

After his friends left, LaRue
heaved the carrot onto the mill.
It buzzed and whirred, cutting the
enormous carrot into lumber.

LaRue put on his tool belt and went straight to work.

First he built a house…

. . . then a boat

and last, a table.

He loaded them onto his big rig and off he went.

LaRue stopped to see **Ivy**

and **Nevil**

and Stella.

Then LaRue found a peaceful
spot to eat the last tiny piece
of the enormous carrot.

It tasted delicious!